Library of Congress Cataloging-in-Publication Data

Yeoman, John.
Old Mother Hubbard's dog takes up sport / John Yeoman and
Quentin Blake.—1st American ed.
p.   cm.
Summary: When Old Mother Hubbard criticizes her dog for being lazy,
he begins playing a variety of sports, creating havoc
around the house and leaving Old Mother Hubbard exhausted.
ISBN 0-395-53361-9
[1. Dogs—Fiction. 2. Stories in rhyme.] I. Blake, Quentin.
II. Title.
PZ8.3.Y460n   1990   89-39942
                                                 CIP
                                                  AC

Printed in Italy
10 9 8 7 6 5 4 3 2 1

Old Mother Hubbard's Dog

Takes Up Sport

John Yeoman & Quentin Blake

Houghton Mifflin Company
Boston 1990

Said Old Mother Hubbard, while combing her hair,
"I don't understand you at all:
You just laze around in a comfortable chair,
While normal dogs play with a ball."

Then, three minutes later
   (it might have been four),
She saw that her troublesome pet
Was playing at tennis against the back door,
With a line of wet clothes for a net.

Said Old Mother Hubbard, "I'm wholly confused!
What is this? It doesn't make sense."
But meanwhile, the dog, looking faintly amused,
Kept pole-vaulting over the fence.

He then got a football, and kicked – with a thud! –
And headed it, higher and higher.
He came in, exhausted, all covered in mud,
And took a hot bath by the fire.

Thought Old Mother Hubbard, while cleaning the bath,
"There's nothing that dog wouldn't dare:
He's speeding on roller-skates right down the path
And doing quick spins in the air."

He went for a jog, and he then had a try
At the long jump, the high jump – the lot.
He picked up the piglets from out of the sty
And practiced at putting the shot.

A little while after, the poor woman froze;
She whispered, "What is he at now?"
The dog was improving his javelin throws
And giving a fright to her cow.

She beckoned him in, barely able to speak,
And settled him down in her lap;
She sighed, "All this energy leaves me quite weak.
I'll teach you a quiet game of Snap."